With love and
best wishes -
from - David
xx

Animal Academy

David R Morgan

David R Morgan

Illustrated by Timothy Joy

Animal Academy

This is a work of fiction.

Library of Congress Control Number: 2020912464

Printed in the United States of America

A 2 Z Press LLC

PO Box 582

Deleon Springs, FL 32130

bestlittleonlinebookstore.com

sizemore3630@aol.com

440-241-3126

ISBN: 978-1-946908--56-8

Dedication

To Bex and Toby,
Who have taught me
more than I'd ever
hoped to learn!

The Manor County School was run by
Mr. and Mrs. Jones and was so fair,

It sat in the middle of sparkling farms
and oh how the children loved it there.

An email arrived saying, *You need more pupils or you'll have to shut down,*
And the children will have to go to the Orwell School ten miles out of town.

Mr. and Mrs. Jones looked so sad.
Then, suddenly, two saucy lambs bounced into the class,
"We'll sit beside Molly Mae," and they smiled as they sprang past.

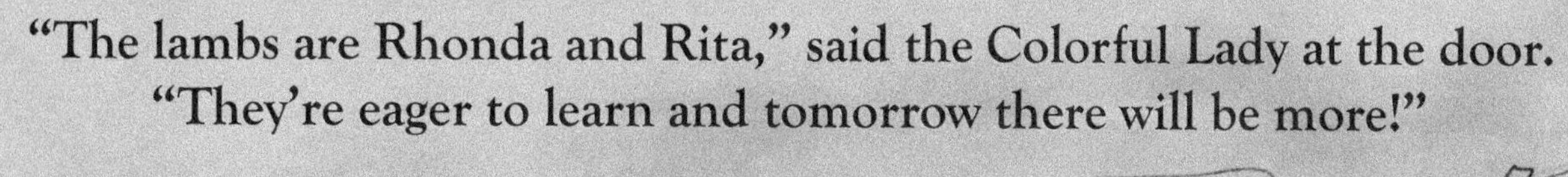
“The lambs are Rhonda and Rita,” said the Colorful Lady at the door.
“They’re eager to learn and tomorrow there will be more!”

As the bell rang on the next day, in came Cauliflower, the singing calf,

And Dodger duckling and Petey the
prancing pony made all the children laugh.

Then came Eustace the clever pig,
Nugget the goat, and Chicken Biddy,
Algebra Rabbit, the math wizz, Robin
the acrobatic fawn, and the
roller-skating Gosling Giddy.

"They are all here on time and eager to learn," said the Colorful Lady. "I'll collect all of them at Home Time, which is half past three."

Everyone's on the register now, as lessons and time passes, the animal pupils had fun at play time and showed such skill in their classes.

But a parent named Mr. Wigan complained, "It's just not right!"
"Having animals and children! I won't put up with this sight!"

And when his son, Matt, said
he's in a Christmas show,
Mr. Wigan was furious,
but was persuaded to go.

Mr. Wigan sat in the audience, complaining to all,
While some others agreed that it was a strange call.

After his son's performance, the two left to go,

And ventured home in Winter's softly swirling snow.

The show carried on so beautifully and it was a big WOW!
The animals and children delightfully displayed their different talents now.

In the end, the whole audience clapped and they cheered,

And they all agreed it was the best
Christmas show in many years and years.

The next term, Mr. Wigan returned with a tiny school inspector,
She inspected the classrooms and gave everything a little score.

And she glanced at the children and animals and gurgled away,

She looked at everything closely on her inspection day.

Everyone showed the tiny school inspector how truly happy they are,

"Hum!" sneered Mr. Wigan. "That won't get you very far."

The tiny school inspector smiled and took off her disguise for all to see,
That she was none other than a very talented inspector turkey.

As the jolly inspector turkey congratulated all, poor Mr. Wigan felt a fool,
The Manor was declared one "OUTSTANDING HAPPY SCHOOL!"

Who could ask for more? Everyone agreed happiness IS outstanding and fun,
And to celebrate, there was jolly tea with delicious donuts for everyone.

In the shimmering summer,
Manor County School received an award,

And became *The Animal Academy* and is so loved and adored.

Now, Tim Wigan returns and finds every day is enchanted,
With joyful learning and perfect play that is so willingly granted.

There are talented animals everywhere and none is a slacker,

Like our very own Governor, who is a gifted alpaca!

So, each new year, children come with birds and sheep and cows,
And the Colorful Lady smiles, and says, "....that is all for now!"

And together they all learned happily every after.

The End

David R Morgan lives in England. He is a talented full-time teacher and writer.

He has written music journalism, poetry and children's books. His books for children include : 'The Strange Case of William Whipper-Snapper', three 'Info Rider' books for Collins and 'Blooming Cats' which won the Acorn Award and was animated for television. He has also written a Horrible Histories biography : 'Spilling The Beans On Boudicca' and stories for Children's anthologies.

For the last 4 years he has been working on his Soundings Project with his son Toby, performing his own poetry/writing to Toby's original music. This work is on YouTube, Spotify and Soundcloud.

Other Books by David R. Morgan

And many more to come!

A2Z Press LLC

A2Z Press LLC
published this work.
A2Z Press LLC is a
publishing company
created by Terrie Sizemore
for the purpose
of publishing literary works by new
and aspiring writers. All content is
G-rated. We welcome your submissions
of ideas for children's literature as well
as adult and self-help topics.
Science and medicine, holidays and
other interesting topics are all welcome.

Submit queries to sizemore3630@aol.com or
PO Box 582
Deleon Springs, FL 32130

Visit our Website

Visit terriesizemorestoryteller.com or bestlittleonlinebookstore.com for our latest titles and gifts for everyone.

Other Books by A 2 Z Press Authors

Eggnog the Bulldog

There is a Poem Inside of Me

How To Succeed In College

H is for Horse

The 23rd Psalm

D is for Dog

Golden Tales: Havoc in Rome

Chilly: The Lost Little Snowboy Ornament

Fairy Hairy Trouble

And More!

Lightning Source UK Ltd.
Milton Keynes UK
UKHW051028040820
367631UK00003B/59